MerCat's Cruise Ship

Adapted by Gabhi Martins

ISBN 978-1-338-88537-8

10 9 8 7 6 5 4 3 2 1 23 24 25 26 27

Printed in the U.S.A. 40

First printing 2023

Book design by Salena Mahina and Two Red Shoes Design

Scholastic Inc.

Look what arrived in the
Meow Meow Mailbox today!
It's a mer-tastic cruise ship!

And it comes with a mermaid horn, too. I know someone who will know just what to do with that. Time to get tiny!

"Who's ready for a mermaid cruise?" MerCat asks as soon as Pandy Paws and I join her in the dollhouse.

Pandy and I reply together: "We are!"

"We're gonna have a whale-of-a-time!" MerCat says.

Then she calls the ship with the mermaid horn. The bathroom rug transforms into water, and a cruise ship rises up!

"Let's get cruising!" Pandy says.

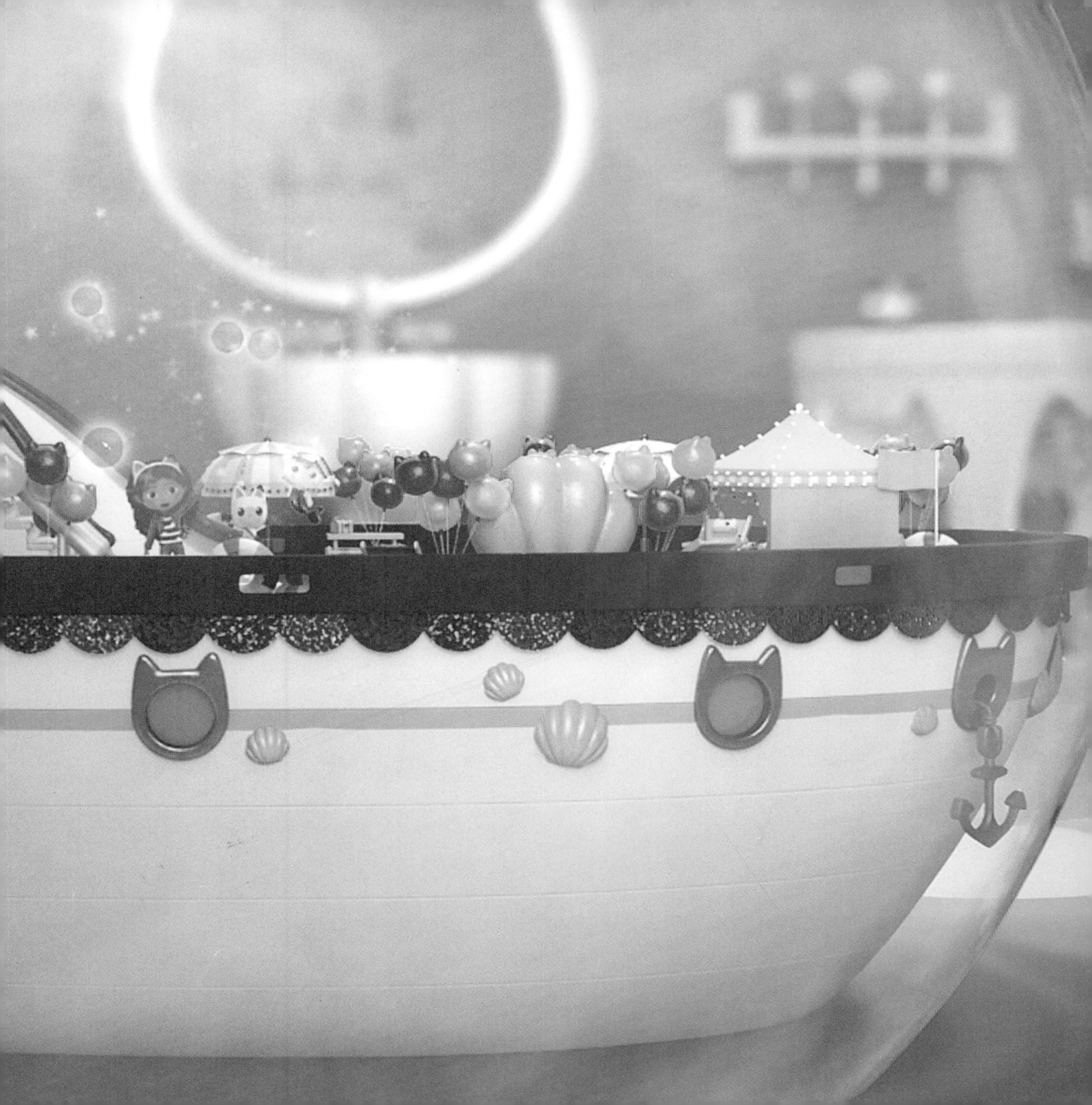

This mermaid ship is a-meow-zing! And another mermaid is coming to meet us . . .

"That's my sister, SunnyCat!" MerCat says. They welcome us to the cruise ship and tell us we'll be doing all sorts of fun activities today.

Baby Box is on the ship, too! Our first activity is making mermaid crowns with her!

"Do you want me to show you how to make one?" Baby Box says and hands us each a vine.

"That would be purr-ific!" I tell her.

Baby Box explains, "Mermaid crowns are made with sea glass, flowers, and shells. You just glue those things onto your vine. Let's get crafting!"

Pandy chooses a shell that's black and white—just like him—for his crown. I choose a piece of sea glass that looks like a purple heart! Then we tie the ends together so we can wear our mermaid crowns.

MerCat announces, "Everyone! It's time to get your tails on!" and then blows the mermaid horn again. We're going to get real mermaid tails!

Pandy Paws goes first. The shell on the Fin Spinner lifts him up. "Oh, they're all so paw-some! I can't decide which fin I want!"

"Don't worry, Pandy. The spinner knows the right fin for you!" SunnyCat says. "Just close your eyes and imagine you're a mermaid."

MerCat spins the wheel and . . . Pandy Paws gets a black-and-white tail just like his shell!

Now it's my turn! The shell picks me up, and MerCat gives me the same tip: "Close your eyes and imagine you're a mermaid. Here we go!"

I get the pink tail! With the pink hearts! “Whoa, I’m a mermaid!”

“You’re mer-mazing!” MerCat says.

“We’ve got two new mermaids in the house! Make a splash!” DJ Catnip calls us to the dance floor. It turns out all the Gabby Cats are on board to celebrate with us!

I turn my hair pink so it matches my mermaid tail, and we dance so much we get hungry. I guess it's time for . . .

"A Mermaid Kitty Treat!" Cakey suggests.

"Oh, that sounds snack-tastic," Pandy Paws says.

We're ready to start making it when another friend comes along. "Can I get in on this snack?" CatRat asks.

"Of course!" we all agree. The more the merrier!

Cakey shows us how to make the Mermaid Kitty Treat. It's a pancake covered in fruit that looks just like a mermaid! My favorite part is the banana scales!

But the most important part is having fun together. Look at our snacks! They look good enough to eat!

We're still finishing our Mermaid Kitty Treats when MerCat appears. "Oh my scales! It's time for our last activity! Swimming with the mermaids!" she says.

The cruise takes us to Mermaid Cove, where we're ready for something magical to happen! MerCat blows her mermaid horn . . .

And mermaid kitties appear!

"Gabby! Pandy! We've been waiting for you! Come swim with us!" the mermaid kitties tell us.

"This is paw-some! I'm going in!" Pandy Paws says. He dives in the water.

Are you ready to see where the mermaids play? Let's go swim together!

Mermaid kitties are magical! There's no place like Mermaid Cove!

Thanks for all your help on our cruise adventure. See you next time!